The Fore Generation

Desiri

The Fore Generation

Desiri

Novelette

Gift Foraine Amukoyo

Soft Grid Limited

Gift Foraine Amukoyo

Published by

Soft Grid Limited

Plot 6, Block 23, Satellite Town

Calabar, Cross River, Nigeria

+234 (0)8027676550, +234 (0)8053110637

E-mail: softgridbooks@gmail.com

softgridltd@hotmail.com

www.softgridbookslimited.com

First Published in 2018

ISBN 978-978-56095-5-4

Soft Grid Books

First Printing, December 2018

For

Onajite Amukoyo

Emmanuel Onomase

Fareedah Usman

CONTENTS

ONE

Mrs Agnes Embarrasses Desiri

Brilliance Primary School was having her final examination for the session. Desiri was in Basic Four. Her classroom was Pink Class.

The pupils came out according to their seat rows to read out from their English Composition textbook. Desiri was shaking in her seat. Her seat was the last on the third row.

When it got to her turn to read, Desiri was sweating. She stood and walked slowly to the front of the class. Her palm was sweaty; she cleaned it on her uniform and nervously held the book in both hands.

"Desiri, we do not have the whole day. Read or you get back to your seat and await zero score." Mrs Agnes said.

Desiri kept staring at the book. She turned over to the next page and pointed at the words. She closed the book and started crying.

"Just go back to your seat. You will fail this. Get out of

my sight." Mrs Agnes said and chewed gum loudly. "All of you should settle down for your written English examination."

Mrs Agnes gave them examination question and answer booklets. She stood in front of the class and asked them to begin. The pupils silently wrote their examination.

Desiri was slow to submit her examination paper. Mrs Agnes called her a 'blockhead' implying Desiri was not brilliant and smart.

Some of the pupils laughed aloud while others smiled at Desiri. Dina felt bad for her friend. She waved at Desiri and mouthed *sorry.* Desiri hiccupped as she walked back to her seat.

Gabriel, a big bully classmate set his leg on her path. He raised his leg a bit high as she came closer. Desiri had begun crying so she did not see the obstacle in front of her.

Desiri's leg bumped into Gabriel's ankle and she was falling. Efe's chair was adjacent to Gabriel's seat. He quickly jumped and caught her arm and the two of them fell to the floor. Gabriel smiled and pretended to be reading his book.

"Thank you Efe, I wasn't watching," Desiri said.

"Of course you weren't watching," Efe murmured, "Ah,

get off me Desiri, your weight is crushing."

"Sorry," Desiri tried to get up and fell on Efe. "Oh, sorry," she clumsily stood up and hopped to her seat.

Gabriel stretched his hand to Efe. Efe held his hand and Gabriel pulled him up.

Efe shook Gabriel's hand and twisted it a little. Gabriel screamed in pain, "You will pay for what you did to Desiri," Efe said.

Gabriel's eyes widened in fright and he stepped backward. He shook his chubby cheeks, "I did nothing," he said.

Efe let go of Gabriel's hand and said, "Relax, not here."

"Is everything okay?" Mrs Agnes asked.

"Yes, y, ye, yes… Ma," said Gabriel.

"Then be on your seats!" Mrs Agnes said.

During break time, Efe brought out four stick of candy from his lunch box and held them between his fingers. The colourful candies attracted Gabriel. He ran to Efe and asked him for a stick.

"Efe, please can I have one candy?"

"No," said Efe.

"Please," Gabriel joined his palms.

"I said no."

"Please, I will do anything you ask of me."

"Really," Efe said and put a candy in his mouth.

Gabriel swallowed, "Yes, I mean it. Please let me have a candy."

"Desiri is very upset. Go over and apologise to her. If she pardons you, then I will give you two candies."

"But I did nothing to her."

Efe raised an eyebrow and pointed to Desiri, "Go now, except you don't want the candies."

"Oh, okay," Gabriel obediently turned around and ran towards her. He apologised to Desiri and she accepted his plea. He happily returned and Efe gave him two candies.

Desiri returned from school, Mrs Tejiri saw how sad Desiri looked. Her mother asked what the trouble was. Desiri kept quiet.

Mrs Tejiri persuaded her daughter to tell her what the matter was. Desiri told her mother what Mrs Agnes had said. Mrs Tejiri was very angry.

The next day, Mrs Tejiri went to the school. She softly spoke to Mrs Agnes but her face showed she was very angry. Mrs Tejiri's complaint drew the attention of the Proprietor, Mrs Yetunde.

Mrs Yetunde was unhappy with Mrs Agnes's remark

about Desiri and she sacked her. This was not the first time Mrs Agnes was rude to a pupil. Twice, she had gotten a suspension for using a board ruler to flog a pupil and insulting a parent.

She pleaded for a third chance but the Proprietor paid Mrs Agnes her salary and asked her to clear out of the classroom. She sadly packed her belongings and left the school.

By the Headmistress instruction, Desiri and her classmates combined with Purple class. They would be with other pupils of Purple Class until the next session when a new teacher would replace Mrs Agnes.

TWO

Desiri Shares Her Fears

Desiri returned from school. She was happy and hugged her mother. Mrs Tejiri asked Desiri about her report card. Desiri gave her mother the envelope contained with her result. Mrs Tejiri went through the result scores and she looked disappointed.

"Desiri, you did not do well in your exams." Mrs Tejiri said.

"No Mommy, I passed. This term, I did not come last in my class." Desiri said excitedly.

"You took the eleventh position out of a total number of fifteen pupils in your class and that is not fair at all. My dear, why do you not try a lot harder to come top in your academics? Make your mommy proud, that way, I will have assurance my child's future will be bright. Desiri, your under-performance in school worries me a lot. All the home tutors I have hired resigned because you never respond to lessons. I cannot teach you myself because I am always busy with work and I don't know much about Mathematics Subject. You want to be an Engineer, right?"

A sparkle came into Desiri's eyes and she happily nodded, "Yes, mommy. I want to fix cars and airplanes."

"But you can't achieve that without quality learning. I am very worried. Desiri, you flop in all subjects. You barely get promoted to higher classes."

Desiri looked downcast. "I am sorry mommy. I can neither read nor spell very well. I want to make you proud. I want to come top in my class, even if it is for once."

"But you are bright my child. I remember the day I went to register you in school. You were so excited and did not want to come home with me. All effort to get you out of the seat was unsuccessful. I had to go home and prepare your meal bag." Mrs Tejiri laughed, "You were so cute and cheerful that your teacher took to you immediately. As you grew older, you began to hate school. Desiri, tell me what are your fears?"

Desiri remained silent and looked up to the ceiling. She switched her foot on the floor, looking sad. It was true Desiri liked school in the past. Her nursery school report cards showed proof of her being one of the best on the graduation list.

In her Basic Class, her attitude towards school changed in a dramatic way. Desiri would cry and roll on the floor during preparation for school.

Mrs Tejiri remembered how Desiri had pretended to be sick. By coincidence, it happened that Desiri had a very high temperature.

She had pulled her school uniform and taken Desiri along to her workplace. She was surprised to see Desiri actively playing around the office without the faintest trace of illness.

Desiri stared shyly, "Mommy."

"Hmmm, yes my dear."

"I wish you can teach me at home. Mommy, I am scared of those teachers. I don't want to go to school any more. They always shout at me, and call me names. Mommy, it could be I do not do well in school because I do not have a father to teach me and take me to school. Efe, the boy that always comes first in my class, his father always drops him off in school. He says his father helps him with all his homework. I think I will do well in Mathematics and other subjects if my daddy was around. Mommy, where is my daddy? Is he dead or alive?" Desiri spoke very fast.

"Desiri," Mrs Tejiri hugged Desiri to her bosom. Desiri

could hear her mother's heart pound Gbim! Gbim! Gbim!

Tears rolled down to Mrs Tejiri's cheeks. It dropped on Desiri's neck.

Desiri freed herself from the tight grip and wiped her mother's eyes with her hands. "Please do not cry mommy. Seeing you cry hurts me more than my failure to excel in my schooling."

"Oh, Desiri, my dearest child, mommy will stop crying now." Again, she hugged Desiri.

THREE

Desiri Tries To Read Aloud

In the night, Desiri stayed awake to read. She opened all her school notes and textbooks on the bed. She glanced from one book to another, trying to figure out why she could not read aloud.

The words were in her mouth. She could tell the meaning of the words, but Desiri could not voice out the words the letters had formed.

Desiri remembered Mrs Agnes's words and she became sad, "I am just a blockhead. I wish my daddy was here to bring down the blocks on my head so that I can learn."

Mrs Tejiri had been peeping at Desiri through the keyhole. She walked fast to her bedroom and gently closed the door. She brought down a big box from top of the wardrobe and took out some pictures.

They were wedding pictures. She hugged the old photos to her bosom and wept.

In the morning, Desiri went about her usual chores. She tidied her room and washed the dishes. Water stopped running in the house. She went outside to fetch water at the tap.

The tap was by their living room's window. Desiri overheard her mother discussing with Mrs Gbenga.

"I am wondering how she conceived the idea that her father's presence will make her study better. I am worried. Desiri is not improving in her studies." Mrs Tejiri said.

"If she is not doing well in formal education, register her in a technical school this holiday season." Mrs Gbenga said.

Mrs Tejiri snapped her fingers, "That is a very good idea. It will come in handy. She will go to a coaching centre from Monday through Thursday, and learn a skill or two during the weekend. This will encourage her in positive ways."

"Yes, this will encourage some positive vibes from Desiri. However, she has every right to know and be with her father. Tejiri, how long will you keep him away from her?"

"Lower your voice…Desiri. She is by the tap and may hear us. Keep your voice down," Mrs Tejiri said.

Few minutes later, Mrs Tejiri and Desiri were alone in the house. Desiri was knitting and singing. Mrs Tejiri suspiciously peered at Desiri through the magazine she was reading. She feared Desiri overhead she and Mrs Gbenga's discussion.

She cleared her throat, "Hum Desiri, Mrs Gbenga had told me something this morning. Hum I cannot remember what it was. Did you hear what she said about Lillian's lunch bag? The bag is so lovely. I would like to get one for you. But I can't remember the name of the shop she bought it from. Can you tell me what you heard about the shop's description? What did she say about the bag?"

Desiri wondered why her mother was lying. "No mommy, I did not hear your discussion with Mrs Gbenga."

"Are you sure? Did you not hear a word? Desiri, please tell me okay, it is for your own good. I want to get the bag for you."

Desiri unhappily stared at her, '*how is keeping my father away from me of any good?*' Desiri thought.

"Desiri, I asked you a question."

She smiled, "Mommy, I did not hear a thing."

"Okay my dearest child. I will go to her house later. I will ask her about the beautiful bag. Finish your knitting. I will serve lunch. You knit beautifully." Mrs Tejiri smiled and touched the stockings, "you knit so neatly."

"Thank you mommy, I will be through in a minute."

Desiri suddenly sat up, "Oh, I want to pee. Excuse me." Desiri dropped her knitting thread and needle on the table. She ran to her bedroom.

"Mom looks relieved. She is happy I did not hear her conversation with Mrs Gbenga. She is happy thinking I know nothing. But I now know a little and it makes me feel sad. My father is somewhere and he has never looked for me. He must hate me so much," Desiri said. She sat on the bed looking very sad. "I want to see you daddy," she cried.

Mrs Tejiri knocked on her door, "Desiri, your lunch is getting cold. Wash your hands properly and come to the dining table."

"Yes mommy, I am coming." she quickly cleaned her tears.

"Come out quickly." Mrs Tejiri said and went to the living room.

Desiri put a smile on her face and came into the living room, "mommy I am not hungry," she said.

"Have you been crying?" Mrs Tejiri asked. Desiri shook her head. "You were crying, baby. Tell mommy what is wrong. Did any of the neighbourhood kids bully you? Did you have a quarrel with your friends?"

"I am fine mommy; tears just dropped," Desiri said.

"Did you cut an onion?" Desiri shook her head. "Of course I know you did not cut an onion. I did the whole cooking. Desiri, why were you crying? You are not telling mommy the truth. I hope you will open up soon."

'I wish you will stop lying and tell me the truth about my daddy.' Desiri thought.

"To brighten your mood, I will make you nice cookies. You will like that, right?"

"Yes mommy, thank you."

"I will bake it right away," said Mrs Tejiri.

"I am coming with you," Desiri walked behind her mother.

"No, you will sit and wait for me. I have a new recipe. I will be making the cookies alone for the first time. It is a surprise," Mrs Tejiri said.

Desiri smiled happily and sat. She drew the password lock pattern on her mother's phone, and searched on children's network to watch kiddies show.

Mrs Tejiri returned, "The cookies will bake for a while and yummy…surprise will be ready!"

Desiri laughed over the phone screen, she peered and saw Desiri was watching a kiddies show on the internet, "Desiri, did you put on my mobile data?" Mrs Tejiri asked.

"No mommy, I did not, your data is off," said Desiri.

"Really," Mrs Tejiri stuck out her tongue and widened her eyes.

"Yes mommy," Desiri laughed over a funny scene. She tumbled backward and laughed harder.

"Careful, don't fall."

"I won't, mommy."

Mrs Tejiri was thoughtful for a while, "I just wonder how you are able to watch the kiddies show online without internet connection."

"You can see for yourself," Desiri said.

Mrs Tejiri checked the phone again. The data was off. She nodded.

Desiri tweaked her nose, "mommy, the cookies are burning!" Mrs Tejiri sniffed and ran to the kitchen.

Luckily, the cookies were not bad. Mrs Tejiri was happy. She deepened the cookies into a small bowl of hot chocolate and served in a tray. Desiri ate one and rolled her eyes.

"Yummy, I want some more, mommy," she licked her fingers.

"Go ahead sweetheart; I baked the cookies just for you."

"Next time, we will bake this together, I want to learn the recipe," Desiri fed her mother some cookies. They watched the kiddies show together. Desiri got two bottles of water from the fridge.

Mrs Tejiri sipped from the bottle of water and ate some cookies, "Desiri, I wonder how you are able to watch movies without internet data."

"I guess they allowed me view it for free because I am a regular customer on the kids' network." Desiri said. Mrs Tejiri laughed. She coughed and drank some water.

At midnight, Mrs Tejiri was trying to access the internet browser on her handheld PC. Google page did not open.

She was confused and decided to check her data balance. It was zero! Mrs Tejiri was shocked. She checked her other phone Desiri had used in the day.

Mrs Tejiri realised the hotspot was turned on. Desiri had been using the data from the handheld PC. She put her head in her palms. Meanwhile, Desiri was smiling in her sleep.

FOUR

Holiday Lessons

The next day, Mrs Tejiri and Desiri went to the Art Centre for Children. She enrolled her into a Graphic Design class. Desiri settled down in her class. Before Mrs Tejiri left, she spoke with the class teacher, Miss Amanda.

After three sessions of colouring and painting exercise, Desiri took permission to go and urinate. She saw some kids rehearsing dance steps in the hallway.

Desiri loved the music they were dancing to and she wriggled her waist to the beat. The way the Dance Department carried out rehearsals thrilled Desiri.

On her way back from the restroom, she stood awhile to watch the dancers. Their legs moved *TAP! TAP! TAP!* She followed their steps for a while and returned to her classroom.

Mrs Tejiri came to pick up Desiri. She told her mother about the dance rehearsals. Seeing her excitement, Mrs Tejiri decided she would register Desiri in the dance department.

Desiri was late for class. She was about to sit when Miss Amanda said, "Desiri, can you remain standing before the class and present your project."

Desiri stepped forward, "yes, Miss Amanda." She was nervous. *'But I am not fully prepared. I should be the Tenth Presenter. I guess my late coming has warranted me an earlier presentation. Desiri, this is your punishment for late coming,'* Desiri thought. She fumbled with her bag and brought out cardboard papers.

Desiri laid out her project on clipping boards. She displayed coloured drawings of a family. Desiri presented that while the mother prepared meal for their lunch boxes, the father polished their shoes. The little kids were happy as their parents drove them to school. The parents said goodbye to their children and drove to work.

The class applauded Desiri's presentation. Desiri beamed. She felt a sense of worth with the ovation. Her school classmates had never applauded her for anything. Desiri was returning to her seat when someone hiccupped.

Her seatmate was crying, "I do not have a father and mother to prepare and take me to school. I have just my grandma and she is too old to even walk me to school. She always tells me that I am not a lucky child. She said my father left my mother when she was pregnant and my mother later left me in her care. Everyone calls me the *Forgotten Child* in my neighborhood," he said.

Desiri turned to Miss Amanda and said, "I do not have a father either. I only wish that family in the drawing was mine."

Miss Amanda came over to comfort them, "Oh, my lovely children. We have plenty daddies and mommies around us." She said. "I am like your mommy, Uncle John is like your daddy," she pointed at her assistant teacher. "We are all parents to you. We can bring you to school, and take you back home, okay. We are here for you. Your daddy is around. Your mommy is around."

"So where is he? I've never seen my daddy," Desiri said.

"Desiri, do not worry. Soon, your daddy will come around and he will bring you to school." Uncle John said.

Desiri shook her head, *'Why will he say my daddy will come around? He does not know anything about my family. Miss Amanda's word did not give me assurance either. My seatmate will not stop crying because his parents are not around. How sad! Well, at least I've got my mommy.'* Desiri thought.

The class closed early. Desiri was happy to resume her exciting dance class. On her way out, Desiri saw Miss Amanda going through her presentation. Miss Amanda smiled at the colourful drawings. Desiri was happy Miss Amanda liked it.

FIVE

25

The Playground

Some people came to visit Mrs Tejiri. From her unhappy expression, it was obvious she did not want them in her house. They greeted good afternoon to one another. Mrs Tejiri opened the door wider for them to come in.

"Desiri, please go to your room," said Mrs Tejiri. Desiri packed up her knitting tools-colourful knitting yarn, needles, scissors, sewing needles, and crochet hook into a fancy basket. She closed the cap of the basket and left.

Later, Mrs Tejiri came to Desiri's room. She sat beside Desiri and told her that those people were her relatives-aunts and uncles.

"Desiri my child, they came because you are the great-great grandchild of their father. He is late and they want you to be at his burial ceremony."

The next day, Desiri's uncles and aunts came to the house. Mrs Tejiri told Desiri to be at her best behaviour. Desiri sat on a small stool in the middle of the room.

One after the other, they placed a gift on Desiri's lap and pecked her on the forehead. Mrs Tejiri took the boxes and put them aside.

After the presentation of gifts, Mrs Tejiri and Desiri escorted the three uncles and three aunts to the door. Mrs Tejiri and one of the aunts spoke in low tones.

Desiri heard an aunt say *'village'*. She wanted to believe they were travelling to the village. She had always told her mother to take her to see her grandparents. Mrs Tejiri always said someday they would go to the village. It seemed now was the time!

Desiri was anxious. She felt certain they would be travelling to the village soon. "I am thinking my aunts and uncles will take me to the village," Desiri said. In the night, she selected her best clothes. Desiri arranged her clothes in a big box.

In the morning, Desiri went to the playground. Every Saturday, all the children in the Estate came out to play. They group into ages and teammates for various sports and games.

The younger girls played inside the bouncing castle and ran around. Some older girls played volleyball. The boys played football and basketball.

Desiri told Lillian about her relatives' visit and future trip to the village. She was excited and hugged Desiri. The boys started cheering Gabriel to jump from a very tall toy horse.

Desiri called out to him, "Gabriel, come down from the horse. You might get hurt!"

"Gabriel, if you don't get off that high horse, you might break your neck," Lillian said.

Gabriel took a deep breathe. The boys cheered him on. He ignored Desiri and Lillian's warning and swung his hands. Desiri closed her eyes while Lillian stood akimbo and twisted her lips. Gabriel somersaulted and crashed to the ground. He broke his arm and cried out in pains.

Desiri called the attention of some adults and they rushed him to the hospital. The children lost interest to play and went to their homes. Desiri was sad.

The Estate's welfare officers sealed up the play area. It was only safe for children to play football and race course on the field, this was more fun for the boys. Desiri became bored.

After coaching hours, there was nothing to do besides watching cartoons. Desiri could not go out to play with most of her friends any more. Sometimes, Desiri and Lillian played hide and seek game in the house. The weeks rolled by. Holiday ended.

SIX

School Resumption

Unlike the eager steps and smiles of most pupils running into the school, Desiri looked sad. She feared school resumption.

Most of the pupils could not wait to write composition on how they spent their long holiday. Any time Desiri walked through the gates, she felt she was going to a cell for some hours. She wished this academic session would end soon.

Desiri saw Efe descending from his father's car. She admired father and son as they hugged each other and shook hands.

"I know he will come top in class. His father always does his homework with him and brings him to school as well." Desiri sighed, "I wish I had a magic wand to fast forward school," Desiri said.

When Desiri took her eyes off her sluggish feet, she realised assembly was over. Some excited pupils dashed around corridors of the classrooms in pairs and in groups.

They chatted as they walked into their various classrooms.

Desiri's lips trembled when Mr Cane walked towards the late comers in his smart and no-nonsense manner. Most pupils considered him as an uncaring man with a predatory frown always registered on his face. The pupils had never seen Mr Cane smile.

Mr Cane shouted, "Wherever you are, on your knees." All the pupils went down on two knees. "Now, move towards the assembly ground, it is time for your own set of morning devotion and be very quick about it," he said.

The pupils crawled on the mowed grass. They were hissing in irritation.

"Do I hear complaints?"

They shouted, "No sir."

"Then move it, move. We do not have the whole day to waste. The last person to reach the assembly ground will get ten strokes of my cane. Do I make myself clear?"

"Yes sir," the pupils shouted and crawled faster.

He waved his cane, "And if you think of coming late again to school this session, you are in for big trouble. Is that clear to you all?"

"Yes sir, we heard you loud and clear, sir." They shouted.

"Now file behind one another according to your heights,"

the pupils were getting up. He stopped them midway. "Everybody down, do that while kneeling!" The pupils assembled as he instructed.

Dina gently elbowed Desiri's arm, "Desiri, why are you among the late comers? I saw you entering the school before end of national anthem," she said.

"I was slow to the assembly ground," Desiri said.

"Oh, well. At least we get to work side by side. I am wondering what today's punishment would be," Dina said.

"But Dina, why are you always late to school? The next building from the school is your house, yet you never meet up school assembly."

"I wake up late."

"Dina, that is because you sleep late. As for me, I have to be up early so that I do not miss the school bus."

"Well, I do not have to hurry to catch the school bus. My house is by the school. I do watch cartoons into the night. It makes me sleep late."

"And your mommy allows you?"

"Yes, my mommy says cartoon makes children smarter," Dina said.

"Yes, watching educative and informative cartoon can make a child smart. Sleeping late is bad. My mommy says early to bed makes one wake up early."

"So how has that helped you? Desiri, you are still the dullest in our class."

Desiri looked downcast, "Yes, I know."

"If you sleep late, you might improve in your academics. No teacher would ever have to call you a blockhead again."

"Dina, do you really think that method would make me brilliant?" asked Desiri.

"Yes, I guess so," said Dina.

"Who are those murmuring?" Mr Cane asked.

Desiri and Dina kept quiet. They quickly drew apart.

"Dina, Desiri, come over here." They crawled towards him. "So, would you pupils like to tell me what you were discussing?" He raised an eyebrow.

"We were not discussing, sir," Dina said.

"Oh, with that loud murmur, you were not discussing. Okay, I have the right punishment for you two. You will go into the toilets and wash it sparkling clean. How the flies buzz around your ears will tell you how loud murmuring irritates me as well. Now march to the toilet blocks."

Desiri and Dina quickly walked down to the toilet while the other late comers laughed at them. Their laughter turned into mumble when Mr Cane asked them to join Desiri and

Dina in the toilet.

At the end of the task, Dina quickly washed her hands and ran off to the classroom. Desiri took more time to wash her hands because she feared going to class and facing the new teacher.

SEVEN

Mrs Bola and Desiri

Desiri came to the classroom and found the new teacher at the board. Mrs Bola was teaching Social Studies. Desiri stood by the door until she finished. On her way to the desk, Mrs Bola saw Desiri.

Mrs Bola cheerfully smiled at her, "I guess you are Desiri." Desiri nodded. "How long have you been standing here?" Desiri raised both hands. "Is it ten seconds?"

Desiri shook her head, "No ma, I stood for ten minutes."

"Were you counting the seconds?"

"Yes ma," Desiri said shyly.

"Okay, I am Mrs Bola. I did not know you were standing there. You should have called my attention. I am not happy you have missed my first subject of the day. Desiri let this be the last time you will be late to school for no tangible reason. I can see you are healthy. Being late to school will not be in my favour and yours too. Do you understand," Desiri nodded. "Come in and take your seat."

"Thank you, Mrs Bola." Desiri quickly walked to her seat.

For the next subject, Mrs Bola shared the pupils' English Composition workbook to them. She instructed them to read from page twenty to twenty-two. She also told them to prepare to tell the class their individual answers.

Desiri started crying. The questions were asking; *'is your father short or tall? What is your mother's favourite meal? How do your parents relate to children, do your parents like being in each other's company?'*

"Desiri, did you get hurt, why are you crying?" Mrs Bola asked. Desiri was quiet. "Class, do you know why Desiri is sad? Can anyone tell me why she is crying?" Mrs Bola persistently asked.

"She does not have a father," Dina said with a sad face.

Mrs Bola took Desiri's workbook and looked over the questions. She read aloud, *what do your parents like doing together. What are your parents' favourite colours?...*

Mrs Bola heard another pupil crying, "Efe, why are you crying?" She asked.

"I don't have a mommy. I cannot answer some questions. I don't know my mother's favourite meal," said Efe.

Mrs Bola sighed tiredly, "Okay pupils, I am going to the

Headmistress's office. Be good boys and girls while I am away. I will be back shortly. Class captain, I want to see the names of noisemakers." Mrs Bola left with the workbook.

Dina brought out the noisemakers' register. She looked at everybody's lips. Dina was keen on writing the names of noisemakers.

Mrs Bola went to the Headmistress' Office. She told her, "The composition workbook was sensitive. The questions were too emotional for some pupils' learning. Madam, they felt sad when they did not have answers to those questions. It affects those that have single parent. It also affects orphans." The Headmistress promised to look into the issue.

Mrs Bola returned to the classroom. She called out names on the class register.

"Ovie Efe," Mrs Bola called.

"Present ma!" Efe said.

"Ovie Desiri," Mrs Bola was surprised.

"Present ma!" Desiri said.

"Efe and Desiri, are you siblings?" Mrs Bola asked. Desiri shook her head.

"No, we are not," said Efe.

"They just have a common surname," said Dina.

"Okay," Mrs Bola said and called other pupils' names.

After school, Dina came to meet Desiri, "Desiri, I have always thought you cannot read. How were you able to understand those words? When I opened the workbook, I knew right away that the questions would hurt you. I am sorry, Desiri."

Desiri smiled at Dina and got into the school bus. She waved at Dina through the window.

EIGHT

Mrs Bola Tells the Pupils a Story

The next day in school, rain was falling heavily. The classroom grew dark and electricity went off. The pupils murmured. They could not see the marker board; it was difficult learning in the dark.

Mrs Bola apologized and stopped writing. She told the pupils it was the end of 'board learning' for the day. She told them a story about the lion.

Desiri put up a hand. "Okay Desiri, you can speak," Mrs Bola said.

"Why is the lion called king of the jungle when he is short in nature compared to other taller mammals? The elephant is much taller and bigger. It gigantic weight can crush the lions' bones to pieces. So why is the mighty elephant not a jungle king?" Desiri asked.

"The lion is vicious than the elephant. It defeats weaker animals with its teeth. It devours big and smaller animals when he is hungry. Most animals are afraid of the lion. Despite the Zebra is taller than the lion, the lion can still bring it to its knees. The lion can eat it up like a common chicken." Mrs Bola said.

"Oh," Desiri said and put her chin on her palm.

Mrs Bola explained the lions' teeth were their strength and pride. They were kings of wild forests. Their viciousness was what scared mild animals. They hung around with dark violence and creepy traits. The heaviest male lion was a king size weighed in Kenya on a scale of two and seventy two kilograms.

Desiri wondered if viciousness was a standard for leadership. There was a rich chief in her neighbourhood who always wore lion's tooth as necklace, and he was very wicked. Desiri paid rapt attention to more stories Mrs Bola had to tell.

NINE

Desiri Vows To Learn

Desiri was knitting a bag on the floor. She was using pink and white thread to weave the bag. Mrs Tejiri and Mrs Gbenga were having a discussion.

"I suffered a lot in my uncle's house. My uncle did not send me to school as he promised my parents. His wife gave me oranges to hawk in the city until I was able to run back to the village. By the time my parents enrolled me in school, my age mates were four classes ahead of me. Now they want my mother's granddaughter because Desiri is an honour to their father."

"My dear, forgive them, forget the past and embrace the future. I am happy for your family and Desiri too. She will attend the ceremony in grand style. You should count your blessing. You are a vessel that bore a great generation." Mrs Gbenga said.

Desiri learned her mother was the great granddaughter of

Pa Ovo.

"Mommy spends so much money on my education and I am yet to make her proud." Desiri said. She went to her room and cried. Desiri became determined to do well in her academics.

Mrs Bola requested Mrs Tejiri's presence in school, "Mrs Tejiri, Desiri has an unusual fear of books. She has biliophobia. She is shy to read aloud and in where two or more persons are gathered, she cannot even utter a word from a book page. I do not know the foundation of her education or upbringing but I think someone had caused her to dislike schooling and books. In this case, it has become difficult to encourage Desiri to read."

"Desiri used to like school."

"She liked attending her crèche and nursery classes, right?"

"Yes, even on weekends, Desiri would cry to wear her uniform to school. She wears her school shoe and carries her lunch bag around the house." Mrs Tejiri and Mrs Bola laughed.

"That was because she was in the class of colours and music-beautiful sights and sounds. At that stage, pupils learn with crayons and watercolours. Every normal child finds the art of colouring object a fascinating exercise. It thrills them to watch cartoons and kiddies songs. However, it is a different procedure in mid nursery and primary where school kids must learn to write and speak properly-spell words and write compositions. How often do you read? Do you read out stories to Desiri?"

"No," said Mrs Tejiri.

"Then you should have some time for that. You need to build an enabling environment for your child to learn. Mrs Tejiri, Desiri should see you read a book. This might peak her interest to be familiar with pages of a book and reading. Read aloud to your child. Children are what they see and hear." She said.

Mrs Tejiri thanked her. She went to another school to get a home tutor for Desiri. She also bought storybooks for Desiri and herself.

TEN

Desiri Learns to Read Aloud

Mrs Bola using phonics primer taught Desiri how to read. During break time, she would list the forty-four sounds in the English language on the board.

She took the lesson through common spelling patterns and pronunciations. Desiri read the list of phonetic related words and spelt words as Mrs Bola spoke.

For emphasis, Mrs Bola mouthed the sounds: */k/ cat and kite, /m/ map, /n/ nest, /s/ sun, /oi/ oil and boy, /ow/ owl and ouch, /urn/ bird and hurt, /u/ yoo…mule, /a/ apple, /e/ elephant, /a/ cake, /o/ boat, /f/ fan, /r/ rat, /z/ zip…* and Desiri repeated the sounds and words after Mrs Bola.

The next day, Desiri met Dina in front of the school gates, "Dina! You are early to school! This is good."

"Yes Desiri, my daddy is back from his long business trip. He stopped me from watching late night cartoons. I can only watch cartoon from 5 pm to 6 pm."

"I am happy you are early to school. Come on, Dina. It is time for assembly," they ran off to the classroom to drop their bags and hurried back to the assembly ground.

Mrs Bola grouped the pupils into different stages of reading group. Sometimes, they held reading sessions under the school' sunshade and formed a round reading circle on the field. Desiri started to read aloud in front of the class.

ELEVEN

Desiri Gets Salute from Soldiers

The Estate's land phone rang. A call came through for Mrs Tejiri. She was not available to take the call. The women were busy training at the military camp. The security in charge of the phone booth met Desiri at the playground. He told Desiri to get her mother to come and return the call. It was an urgent call from her office.

The Military Camp was few walk from the Estate. Desiri was happy to come out. She only got to see the roadside when she went to school, church or an outing with her mother.

Desiri entered the Army Camp through the pedestrian gate. A motorcyclist drove his noisy bike pass the office of a Senior Army Officer. The soldiers on guard stopped and punished the bike man for riding a noisy bike. They asked him to do frog jump.

"Next time, you will not bring a noisy machine into a

military camp," said a soldier.

The National Anthem recitation boomed from the camp's trumpets. Desiri knew the rules. She stood at attention. After National Pledge, she excitedly rushed off to look for her mother.

She shouted, "Mommy Desiri," and waved her hands for her mother to sight her.

Mrs Tejiri took permission from her coach. She changed badge with another football player and left the field.

Mrs Tejiri cleaned her sweaty face with a small towel, "Desiri, what are you doing here?"

Desiri copied the footballers. She pretended to be playing ball, "There is a call from your office. The Security Guard asked me to call you."

"Oh, my phone must have been ringing in my bag," Mrs Tejiri picked up her bag amongst other bags on the ground. "Come on, Desiri." Desiri took the bag and hanged it on her shoulder.

Desiri and Mrs Tejiri bade some neighbours' goodbye. They exited the training ground in a hurry. They took the second gate because it was a faster route to reach the Estate's small gate. On their way out, they saw a defaulter who had walked on while the anthem was being song.

A Soldier gave the old man a very short broom to sweep from the gates to the Officers Mess. It was a long distance in-between. "Sweep it very well you bloody disrespectful civilian!" he said.

Desiri felt pity for the old man. She told Mrs Tejiri to wait and ran to the old man. Desiri took the broom from him and started sweeping. The Soldier felt bad for punishing the old man. He collected the broom from Desiri and asked the old man to go. Another Soldier praised Desiri for been a good and thoughtful child. The Soldiers gave her a salute.

TWELVE

Father's Day

Today was father's day. Mr Gbenga returned home with chicken and chips.

Lillian ran to her father. She hugged him and said, "Happy Father's Day, daddy!"

Desiri was sad. She turned to leave.

"Desiri, how are you?" Mr Gbenga asked.

"I am fine, Mr Gbenga," said Desiri.

"Desiri, will you not give me a hug to celebrate father's day?"

Desiri hugged him. "Happy father's day, Mr Gbenga, I wish you all the best." Desiri offered him a knitted stocking.

Mr Gbenga admired the beautiful stockings, "Oh, this is beautiful."

"I am sorry, Mr Gbenga. It is not your size. Oh, well. I did not know today is father's day. I would have made something of your size. You will not be able to wear this."

"Oh, Desiri, my dear, I will be the one to wear it."

"How will you wear it? It is small to fit your feet."

"I will give it to my granddaughter."

"Will you give the socks to your granddaughter?" Desiri asked.

"Yes, Aunt Temi will come to the house with her little baby. She is coming over for Mrs Gbenga to look after her and the baby."

"I thought Mrs Gbenga will go over to her house to take care of them." Desiri said.

"Yes, but Mrs Gbenga is not very strong to travel. Aunt Temi will come here and stay for three months. That will give you and Lillian enough time to play with the baby. I am sure you are happy about that." Desiri and Lillian jump excitedly.

"I will also knit a matching cap and sweater for the baby," Desiri said and ran home in anticipation.

Desiri knitted baby kits and sang, '*I am knitting to keep baby warm…warm, warm, warm…I cannot wait to see baby see, see, see...*' When she finished knitting, Desiri looked at her work with satisfaction.

Mrs Tejiri came into the living room. She congratulated Desiri for a job well done.

Mr Gbenga received his grandchild and daughter. Lillian came to inform Desiri of their arrival. Desiri packed the items in a fancy bag and went with Lillian. Desiri presented her gift to aunt Temi. They were thankful for the beautiful costumes.

Mr Gbenga gave Desiri some money but she refused in a polite manner.

"No sir. I will not collect money for the gift items. I have given to the baby with love." Desiri said.

Aunt Temi patted Desiri's hand, "you are a nice child. Thank you, Desiri. You can hold the baby." She carefully gave the baby to Desiri. Lillian supported Desiri to carry the baby for a while. Desiri pecked the baby before aunt Temi took her.

THIRTEEN

Desiri Meets Her Grandparents

Mrs Tejiri and Desiri journeyed to the village. Desiri was happy to be on the road trip. She asked her mother about the big rocks and wild forests she was seeing on the roadsides. She saw a boy come out of the forest. "Mommy, I saw a boy riding a bicycle. Do people live in the bush?"

Mrs Tejiri looked out the window and saw the little active boy. He was pushing a bicycle load of palm fruits, "Desiri, beyond the city, there is also a beautiful village life. There are farms in the bushes. The soil in the forest can be more fertile. This may cause farmers to plant their crops in the forest." Desiri nodded and kept on staring at the boy.

There was traffic jam. They were stuck in a hold up. Desiri admired the way the boy rolled his old bicycle ahead of their car. They stopped at an eatery. Desiri saw the boy selling his palm fruits. She drew her mother's attention and Mrs Tejiri bought some of the fresh palm fruits.

They reached the village and Desiri stared at the older version of her mother.

Desiri ran into the old woman's opened arms, "Grandma, grandma, I am pleased to meet you. After so many years, I finally get to see you in real. Mommy only showed me pictures of you and grandpa." Desiri bobbled in her grandmother's arms.

"I have missed you my lovely grandchild. Tejiri, thank you for coming, I was uncertain if you had forgiven your uncle and aunt. I thought you would not make it to the burial ceremony." Grandma Fejiro said.

"No Mama, I cannot. I forgave them a long time ago. I could not go to such extent," said Mrs Tejiri.

She walked to her mother in slow motion. She hugged her from behind with a passion that showed how much she missed her mother. Tears dropped on Desiri's forehead. She looked up to see her grandmother crying.

"Please grandma, you are crying," Desiri said. She wiped the tears from her cheeks.

"Yes my lovely grandchild, but these are tears of joy. After nine years, your mother brings you to see me. The last time I held you, you were so little. You were a month old when I last carried you in my arms," With a lot of effort, the old woman jerked Desiri up.

Desiri held on tight to her grandma's shoulders and Mrs Tejiri supported her mother by holding Desiri. They went into the house. Their young relatives followed behind with their luggage.

Desiri knelt, "Degwo-I am on my knees grandpa," she greeted her grandfather in their ethnic language.

"Vrendo my dear," Grandpa Fejiro replied. He patted Desiri's shoulder and lifted an eyebrow in surprise. "The city parents teach their children the language of our forefathers? Oh, this is splendid, may we praise the gods." Grandpa Fejiro said.

"Yes Papa, I speak the language to her. From the moments of my pregnancy, I sang and spoke to her in our language. Desiri can speak well," Mrs Tejiri said. She knelt before her father, "degwo Papa."

Grandma Fejiro brought food-starch and Banga soup. Desiri and Mrs Tejiri ate in delight. The family caught up on old times.

They ate fruit salad as they discussed. Desiri noticed grandpa Fejiro scratched his head so much. The white hair fascinated her. They were short and curly.

"Grandpa, you are scratching your head so much. Tell me

why you beat your hair?" asked Desiri.

"My dear grandchild, you will get to my age and come to know the reason," said Grandpa Fejiro. He smiled.

FOURTEEN

Desiri Meets Her Father and Brother

They had some visitors. Grandma Fejiro ushered them into the house. Desiri was the first to see Efe and his father. Mrs Tejiri stopped eating when she saw them. She ran towards Efe and hugged him. She looked at his face and hugged him again.

Desiri was openmouthed when Mr Ovie, Efe's father lifted her into his arms. "Are you my uncle?" Desiri asked him.

"Desiri, you are in your father's arms. Efe is your brother," said Grandma Fejiro. Desiri's eyes widened.

Efe was Desiri's younger brother. Mrs Tejiri and Mr Ovie were their parents. The family separated when the children were little.

The grandparents took Mrs Tejiri and Mr Ovie to another room. Grandpa Fejiro counselled them about distance, which was not good for their children's upbringing. Grandma

Fejiro joined Mrs Tejiri and Mr Ovie's hands together. However, the couple did not look happy.

The family went for a picnic. While playing with other children, Desiri fell into the river. Her parents panicked and called for help. Desiri emerged from the river. A bear carried her on its back. The bear dropped her by the riverbank and returned to the water.

"Thank you, Mr Bear," Desiri said. She waved at the bear and her mother wrapped a towel around her body.

FIFTEEN

15

The Bear and Desiri

On the day of Pa Ovo's burial, a bear came out to pay tribute to Pa Ovo. The same bear saved Desiri from drowning. The bear usually protect the people from drowning in the river and come out to honour dead oldest people of the village.

The bear rounded the coffin seven times. It strode to the bush and returned with a beautiful chair attached to its back. The bear's guards carried Desiri and Efe onto the seat. The bear danced around to the music from the guards' flutes.

The performance excited Desiri. She danced and waved a white handkerchief in the air and at the people. The bear danced towards the burial reception ground. A Guard put them down. The guards strolled with Desiri and Efe to the table with drinks.

"The bear is thirsty; it wants a drink," the Guard said.

The elders nodded at Desiri. She jumped in excitement. Desiri took a pack of juice and went to the bear. The bear opened its mouth. Desiri poured the juice into the bear's mouth and Efe did the same.

The bear danced around and headed towards the bush. The bear's guards played flute and danced behind the bear. Desiri and Efe received attention from many relatives and townspeople; they presented gifts and money to them.

The Master of the Ceremony said, "Pa Ovo is a very fortunate man. We thank God for a life well spent. Dear beloveds of Pa Ovo, I see some of you crying, and I want to believe it is tears of joy. Today's occasion is a celebration of life. He died the oldest man of this village and has great-great grandchildren. Where are they? Let the distinguished children come forward."

An escort ushered Desiri and Efe to a big chair. Some dignitaries of the community and royal chiefs flanked Desiri and Efe.

"Do you see how majestic Pa Ovo's fore generations look? He must feel fulfilled among his ancestors," said the MC. The people nodded and clapped. Dancers performed Udje dance. The celebration ended.

Mr Ovie and Efe arrived very early on Monday morning. Desiri and Efe accompanied their grandparents to the farm. They uprooted tubers of cassava. Desiri and Efe carried some cassava in a small basket and chatted on their way home. Grandpa Fejiro and grandma Fejiro were happy and grateful their grandchildren were around to help.

At home, they peeled the cassava tubers and put in large bowls. Grandma Fejiro, Desiri and Efe washed the cassava tubers while Mrs Tejiri and Mr Ovie mashed the cassava tubers in a mortar. Grandma Fejiro mixed the mash cassava with palm oil, which would produce yellow garri or oil garri.

Afterwards, some workers arrived. They put the mixed mashed cassava in a sieve-like bag and placed each bags in different press machines. Excess starchy water began to drip from the bag.

They allowed the starchy water to drip for over three hours. When the cassava became dry, the workers came to set large clay frying pan on tripod with burning firewood.

Mrs Tejiri and grandma Fejiro filtered and began to fry the dried cassava on the hot pan. Desiri and Efe washed the bowls, swept and packed the cassava peels into a bag. They were happy doing the chores.

After the vacation, Mr Ovie and Efe went back to the city. Desiri was sad. She missed her father and brother.

"Tejiri, I thought after spending time with your husband, both of you will reconcile for the sake of the children. Why are you being stubborn?" said grandma Fejiro.

"Mama, it will take me time to accept him back. He decided to pursue his career in another country. He left me when I needed him the most. I just need some time," said Mrs Tejiri.

"Tejiri, you still need him. Do not take forever to come to a decision. Time does not wait for anyone. Desiri was very sad after Ovie and Efe left. Tejiri, don't be selfish, think about your son and daughter." Grandma Fejiro said.

"Yes Mama. Please go to bed." Grandma Fejiro nodded and went into the bedroom.

Mrs Tejiri and Desiri left the village two days later.

SIXTEEN

Family Reunion

Mr Ovie visited Mrs Tejiri. Desiri was happy to see her father. She took him to her bedroom.

"Daddy, this is my room."

"I know, my dear. I built this house. Your mother and I used to live here. Efe was also born here before we left Nigeria."

Desiri was very surprised, "Why is it that I don't remember anything?" she asked.

"Child, you were a little baby," said Mr Ovie.

Desiri made her father sit on the bed and showed him her baby pictures. Tears fell from Mr Ovie's eyes. He was happy to see the babyhood memories of his daughter. Desiri was two year old when he and Mrs Tejiri had separated. He took Ovie with him to live in London. Desiri cleaned his tears. He hugged her very tight.

Mrs Tejiri came into Desiri's room. She was tearful

seeing father and daughter. She ran to Mr Ovie. Mr Ovie opened his arms wide and they hugged one another. Desiri happily wrapped her arms around her parents.

Desiri and her mother went to the market. They bought traditional beads. The seller clipped some cowries to Desiri's hair. The woman showed her the new look in the mirror. The beautiful reflection awed Desiri.

The woman wore a cowrie bracelet on Desiri's wrist. Desiri loved them and refused to take the costumes off. Mrs Tejiri paid for them and bought some beads for Efe. The sales woman thanked them for their patronage.

She gave Desiri a cowrie necklace as parting gift and appreciation for the patronage.

They took the materials to an African tailor. The Designer took measurements of Desiri and her mother. She gave them a date to pick up the clothes. Desiri was happy.

Desiri's father and brother came to live in the Estate. Her parents held a birthday party for her. It was a double celebration to celebrate Desiri for taking the fourth position in her class and for Efe coming first.

The birthday theme was a costume party. The children and adults wore African attires. It was a colourful celebration with much food to eat and juice to drink.

Desiri's friends performed the Udje dance. They had practiced the steps under the guidance of Desiri's mother. Desiri was happy seeing a miniature performance she had enjoyed in the village. She joined her friends and followed the steps.

Desiri ran to Mrs Tejiri, "Mommy, please you will teach me more dance steps for my cultural day at school?"

"Yes Desiri, I will teach you many dance steps," said Mrs Tejiri.

SEVENTEEN

Dele Goes To School

A boy watched Desiri as she walked out from the library with books in her hand. He was walking with his parents to the Proprietor's office.

His cornrows-hair braids enthralled Desiri. She had heard it was natural for the descendants of Sango to plait their hair. She wanted to have another look at the beautiful woven locks and she followed them.

The boy and his parents sat in the office. He kept throwing inquisitive glances at Desiri. Mrs Yetunde and his parents discussed for a while.

"I am sorry, madam. We cannot admit your child into our school. If he wants a place here, then he has to cut his hair."

The descendants of Sango had not been receiving formal education in Nigeria. Dele and his parents had relocated from America. His parents had come to register him in the school.

The Alaafin of Oyo-the ruler of Dele's ethnic community had made it possible for them to attend school within the community. He built schools where Sango descendants received formal education. Dele's parents could not take him there because they had their jobs in this city.

Mr and Mrs Bode could not apply for transfer at their new job. They could only do that after three years. They were sad their child would only have a home tutor.

After knocking, Mrs Yetunde asked Desiri to come in. She walked into the Proprietor's office in a bold manner. Desiri held Dele's hand. They walked hand in hand and stood in front of Mrs Yetunde, "No, you cannot deny Dele a formal education." Desiri said.

The statement startled Mrs Yetunde, "Desiri, you can't tell me what to do." She said.

"Please, Mrs Yetunde. If Dele does not get this admission, he will be unhappy at home. Look at his parents; you can see they are sad. Mrs Yetunde, Dele was a pupil in the United States of America. Would it not be a shame that he cannot go to school in his fatherland. We have a pupil; a boy that has a long hair in this school."

In quick defence, Mrs Yetunde said, "Jake is a foreigner, he is American and they grow long hair in that nature."

"So also is Dele. Dele is a descendant of Sango. His locks are natural. He is a Nigerian and deserves formal education here in Nigeria, in this school."

Mr and Mrs Bode nodded in agreement. Dele looked at Desiri with admiration.

Mrs Yetunde thought for a while, "Congratulations! Welcome to our school, Dele Bode. You can resume today, if that is okay." She smiled.

Mr and Mrs Bode were happy. Desiri shook Dele's hand. Dele was very excited.

Dele resumed school immediately. Mrs Yetunde introduced him to the class. The pupils welcomed him with vibrant applause. Gabriel waved one hand and smiled.

Dele's seat was in front of Desiri and his seatmate was Efe. He looked backward. Dina waved at him. Dele and Desiri smiled at each other.